CHICAGOLAND
DETECTIVE AGENCY
N° 2

The Maltese Mummy

TRINA ROBBINS
ILLUSTRATED BY TYLER PAGE

GRAPHIC UNIVERSE™ • MINNEAPOLIS • NEW YORK

STORY BY **TRINA ROBBINS**

PENCILS AND INKS BY **TYLER PAGE**

LETTERING BY **ZACK GIALLONGO**

Graphic Universe™
A division of Lerner Publishing Group, Inc.
241 First Avenue North
Minneapolis, MN 55401 U.S.A.

Website address: www.lernerbooks.com

Library of Congress Cataloging-in-Publication Data

Robbins, Trina.
    The Maltese mummy / by Trina Robbins ; illustrated by Tyler Page.
       p. cm. — (Chicagoland Detective Agency ; #2)
    Summary: As the founders of the Chicagoland Detective Agency, a haiku-writing girl and a boy with a talking dog have more than enough cases on their hands (and paws) when a friend vanishes, a mummy's amulet disappears, and an evil scientist stalks human brains and hearts.
      ISBN: 978–0–7613–4615–9 (lib. bdg. : alk. paper)
      1. Graphic novels. [1. Graphic novels. 2. Mystery and detective stories.
3. Mummies—Fiction. 4. Egypt—Antiquities—Fiction. 5. Chicago (Ill.)—
Fiction.] I. Page, Tyler, 1976– ill. II. Title.
PZ7.7.R632Mal 2011
741.5′973—dc22   2010028273

Manufactured in the United States of America
2 – BC – 9/1/11

7

THE STEPFORD SENTINEL
Bringing You All the News from Stepford Preparatory Academy

Sun D'Arc in Chicagoland for World Tour!

by Class President Sylvia Martin

The halls of Stepford Prep are seething with excitement because superstar singer Sun D'Arc is coming to our own Chicagoland! Mr. D'Arc's manager, Vora Schak, has sent two tickets to the journalism department of every Chicagoland high school, inviting teen reporters to a special school newspaper conference before his show. Mr. D'Arc has a special bond with all teenagers because, at 18, he is still a teen himself. Stepford Prep will be represented at the conference by our beloved poetry editor, Megan Yamamura, and a friend.

No Running on Stairs

by Class President Sylvia Martin

Yesterday, one of our students, Otto Van Blick, was injured when two students running on the stairs knocked into him. Otto suffered a sprained wrist and was sent home, where we all hope he recovers quickly. The two students, who shall remain nameless, were also sent home, where we hope they will meditate on the damage they have done. We hope that all the students will learn from this sad lesson: running on the stairs is dangerous and can lead to sprained wrists and other disorders.

Otto's mother, Mrs. Van Blick, hopes that one of Otto's friends will bring him his homework.

Two Haiku on Sun D'Arc

by Megan Yamamura, poetry editor

I
O Sun, shine D'Arcly!
Your guitar sadly whimpers
Singing its sorrow.

II
O Sun, my dark moon!
Only I, a teenaged girl,
Share your suffering.

INQUIRING REPORTER

by Class President Sylvia Martin

This week's Inquiring Reporter question is:

When our school has special tickets to give out for major events, like, for instance, a press conference with a cool rock star, do you think it's fair that the teachers can decide who to give the tickets to, just because, say, somebody wrote a poem or something, or should there be a lottery, so everybody has a chance?

Your opinions will be printed in the next issue.

Introducing Jazmin Farid!

by Class President Sylvia Martin

We hope everybody at Stepford Prep will give a rousing welcome to our new student Jazmin Farid. Jazmin hails all the way from sunny Egypt. Jazmin's faves are rocky road ice cream, long walks on the beach, and the superstar singer Sun D'Arc. Let's all show Jazmin that famous Stepford hospitality!

Bradley: Dames! You can never trust them.

Megan: Only friend? What am I, chopped liver?

Megan: SO, RAF, BECAUSE YOU'RE MY *ONLY FRIEND,* DO YOU WANNA COME WITH ME SATURDAY TO SEE SUN D'ARC? THEY'RE HOLDING IT EARLY IN THE DAY SO IT CAN BE KIDS-ONLY. IT'LL BE AWESOME!

Megan: OF COURSE YOU'RE MY FRIEND, BRADLEY. BUT YOU'RE, LIKE, A *DOG.*

Bradley: Never mind me, I'm just a dog, my feelings don't get hurt.

Raf: AWESOME, RIGHT?

Bradley: I'll just stay home alone tomorrow and read The Maltese Falcon.

Raf: Been meaning to read it.

Raf: UM, MEGAN, *ACTUALLY,* I NEVER *HEARD* OF SUN D'ARC. BUT I'D LIKE TO GO AND FIND OUT WHAT EVERYBODY SEES IN HIM.

Megan: WOW, RAF, YOU ARE THE PRINCE OF NERDS! LOOK, HERE'S SUN D'ARC'S *MYBLOGFACE* PAGE--AND *I'M* ON IT!

MYBLOGFACE

Meet the FACE

Sun D'Arc
Age: 18 years old but with a 2,000-year-old soul.

"The world is my home, and all its sorrow."
Latest hit: "U Fly With Me, Broken Bird."

Friendly FACErs

90,233,960 Friends

Altadonna   London

Tiffni   Annie Missouri

Sun D'Arc's Bio

Interests:
Meditating on the sorrows of a foolish world, black lace on my shirts made to order by nuns at a convent in the south of France, watching the crows flock at eventide along the Thames, reading the obituaries, black boots custom made in Italy, long walks on the beach, and rocky road ice cream.

Sun D'Arc Check out my new vid for "U Fly With Me, Broken Bird." Peace.

September 6 at 1:15 PM

 London: I love you, Sun D'Arc, but please give back my daddy's hotel. I didn't mean to give it to you for keeps, it was only a loan, and Daddy's asking about it.

 Altadonna: Do you think you could go for an older woman?

 Tiffni: You promised we had a date. Why did you stand me up? My heart is breaking!

 Annie Missouri: I never knew the delicious torture of love till I met you!

 Megan Yamamura: Hi, it's me, Megan! I'm your biggest fan and I've sent you six hundred haiku!

The best laid plans of dog and boy aft gang aglay.

WHAT DOES *THAT* MEAN?

It means Raf has the flu and can't go with you today.

ID'S TRUE. AAAAH.

BUT WHAT'LL I *DO*? IF I GO ALONE, I'LL LOOK *PATHETIC* AND EVERYONE WILL *KNOW* I'M TOO WEIRD TO HAVE ANY FRIENDS.

I COULD INVITE THAT HORRIBLE *JAZMIN*, WHO TRIED TO WORM A TICKET OUT OF ME, BUT I'D RATHER DIE.

...CHOOOO!!!!...

HI, RAF. HI, MEGAN.

MY MOM SENT OVER SOME OF HER SPECIAL GUMBO, WHICH SHE SAYS IS HOT ENOUGH TO CURE *ANYTHING.*

WILLIAM!

I HAVE TWO TICKETS TO A PRESS CONFERENCE WITH SUN D'ARC BEFORE HIS CONCERT. YOU WANNA COME *WITH* ME?

REALLY? SUN D'ARC IS A *SUPERSTAR!* SURE, THANKS!

GUESS I'LL SPEND THE EVENING WITH *PBS*. THERE'S A *SPECIAL* ON ABOUT THAT MUMMY AT THE *ART INSTITUTE*.

ID WOULD BE DICE TO HAVE A REPORT ON THE PRESS CONFERENCE, THOUGH...

Sigh...

I'LL TELL YOU ALL ABOUT IT. I BET MY MOM'LL LET ME STAY OVER IF WE SAY IT'S TO HELP YOU CATCH LIP WITH HOMEWORK.

SO CAN I, MOM? *THANKS!*

AAAAH...

C'MON, C'MON, WE HAVE 45 MINUTES!

SHADDUP

blink

blink

blink

SHE LOOKS FAMILIAR.

TAP TAP

THAT'S BETTER. NOW, I'M *VORA SCHAK,* SUN D'ARC'S *MANAGER.* YOU CAN EACH ASK SUN *ONE* QUESTION...

...EH?

TWO HOURS LATER.

THIS WAY.

O Sun, thy sweet sounds, Music of love and sorrow, Speak only to moi.

I COULDN'T *HEAR* ANYTHING, EVEN FROM BACKSTAGE. ALL THOSE GIRLS WERE SCREAMING!

NO!!!!!

I SAID NO!!!!!

NO SODA, NO LEMONADE, NO ICED TEA! WHERE IS MY SPECIAL HERB TEA! I TELL YOU, I *MUST* HAVE MY SPECIAL HERB TEA. DO YOU *HEAR* ME?

Argh...

SUN! *CALM* YOURSELF. OUR, ER, *GUESTS* ARE HERE.

EH?

OH! HEH.

DO COME IN. SUN IS VERY *DELICATE* AND *SENSITIVE*, YOU KNOW.

AH YES, DO HAVE A SEAT. WHAT DID YOU SAY YOUR *NAME* IS?

WILLIAM.

SUN, COULD YOU TELL THE STUDENTS OF STEPFORD PREP ABOUT YOUR LOVE OF CRO--

A *SODA*, WARREN? I THINK WE STILL HAVE A GLASS THAT SUN DIDN'T BREAK. HOW *OLD* ARE YOU, WARREN?

TWELVE. WILLIAM.

SUN, THE STUDENTS WOULD LOVE TO KNOW THE INFLUENCES IN YOUR--

HOW *TALL* ARE YOU EXACTLY, WILBUR?

UM, FIVE FEET SIX INCHES?

I BET YOU HAVE A *FASCINATING* FAMILY BACKGROUND, WESTON.

WE'RE FROM CHICAGO.

FURTHER BACK THAN THAT.

WILLIAM.

THE *MUMMY!* THE MUMMY WAS WEARING THAT AMULET!

LOOK, I'LL RERUN IT AND *SHOW* YOU.

AS THE MUMMY OF RA-HOTEP IS CAREFULLY UNWRAPPED, DRS. WEDGELEY AND STARBUCK MAKE AN AMAZING DISCOVERY: A UNIQUE JEWEL-ENCRUSTED GOLDEN *AMULET,* OF SUPERIOR CRAFTSMANSHIP, PLACED ABOVE THE HEART. SINCE RA-HOTEP'S HEART HAS OF COURSE BEEN *REMOVED* FROM HIS BODY, IT IS BELIEVED THAT THIS AMULET IS MEANT TO SERVE AS THE MUMMY'S *NEW HEART.*

SEE THE *CRACK* RUNNING THROUGH THE AMULET AND THE *CHIP* ON ONE SIDE? IT'S THE *SAME* AMULET THAT SUN D'ARC IS WEARING IN YOUR PHOTO.

MEGAN, YOUR ROCK STAR IS A *JEWEL THIEF*. HE CAME TO CHICAGOLAND TO *STEAL* RA-HOTEP'S AMULET FROM THE MUSEUM!

NONSENSE! SUN D'ARC IS *FILTHY RICH*. HE PROBABLY HAD THE AMULET *COPIED*.

This is just like in the book I'm reading, where the detective is looking for a priceless, stolen ancient work of art: the jewel-encrusted golden statue of a falcon.

RAF, WHAT ARE YOU DOING?

GOTTA GET *DRESSED*. WE'RE GONNA GO TO THE ART INSTITUTE AND SNEAK A LOOK IN RA-HOTEP'S *SARCOPHAGUS*.

IF THE AMULET IS *MISSING*, WE'LL KNOW SUN D'ARC *STOLE* IT!

BUT, RAF, YOU'RE *SICK*.

FEELING *MUCH* BETTER!

Woof! This is just like in the book! Now, this looks like a case for the Chicagoland Detective Agency!

BUT WE STILL HAVE TO FIND *WILLIAM*!

EASY-PEASY. WE TEXT HIM EVERY *FIFTEEN MINUTES*. EVENTUALLY, HE'S *BOUND* TO ANSWER! CASE SOLVED!

CHAPTER THREE:
MUMMY ON THE MOVE!

THE FAMOUS ART INSTITUTE MUSEUM.

THE SARCOPHAGUS ROOM IS CLOSED. NOW WHAT?

GIVE ME A MOMENT TO THINK... WE'LL WAIT UNTIL RIGHT AFTER CLOSING TIME, WHEN THERE'S NO ONE AROUND, AND SNEAK IN.

IF YOU SEE THE AMULET IS THERE, YOU'LL GO HOME AND REST, RIGHT?

RIGHT.

MEGAN? FROM *SCHOOL?* WHAT ARE *YOU* DOING HERE?

I MIGHT ASK *YOU* THE SAME QUESTION, JAZMIN. WHAT ARE *YOU* DOING IN A SECRET TUNNEL BENEATH THE MUSEUM?

ACTUALLY, IT'S *INSPECTOR* JAZMIN FARID, OF THE *CAIRO EGYPTIAN ANTIQUITIES DEPARTMENT.*

INSPECTOR...? BUT YOU'RE JUST A *KID!*

ACTUALLY, I'M 20 YEARS OLD. I'M THE *YOUNGEST* AND *SHORTEST* MEMBER OF THE ANTIQUITIES DEPARTMENT, WHICH HAS MADE IT EASY FOR ME TO POSE AS A HIGH SCHOOL STUDENT AND *INFILTRATE* HIGH SCHOOLS ACROSS THE COUNTRY.

WE'VE BEEN TRACKING A NOTORIOUS *GANG* THAT HAS BEEN FOLLOWING THE MUMMY OF RA-HOTEP ACROSS THE COUNTRY. AND NOW THEY HAVE FINALLY *STOLEN* THE MUMMY.

THERE WERE OTHER RUMORS, BUT I BELIEVE THE *LEADER* OF THE GANG, A FIENDISH *JEWEL THIEF* AND NOW A *MUMMY THIEF* TOO, IS NONE OTHER THAN *SUN D'ARC!*

MY BELOVED SUN D'ARC? *NO WAY!*

WAY. SUN D'ARC HAS PERFORMED IN *EVERY CITY* WHERE THE MUMMY HAS BEEN EXHIBITED, WAITING FOR A CHANCE TO *STEAL* IT.

AFTER THE SHOW, I TRACKED HIM TO THIS *SECRET TUNNEL.*

WE DON'T KNOW *WHY,* BUT FOR SOME REASON *HIGH SCHOOL STUDENTS* ARE NECESSARY TO THE GANG'S PLAN.

IN *EVERY* CITY WHERE HE PLAYS, SUN D'ARC INVITES HIGH SCHOOL STUDENTS TO A *PRESS CONFERENCE.* THAT'S WHY I HAD TO GO TOO.

BUT WHY COULDN'T THE ANTIQUITIES DEPARTMENT JUST *BUY* YOU TICKETS TO THE SHOW?

I...WELL, I WOULDN'T HAVE MINDED GOING WITH A FRIEND, FOR ONCE.

LIGHTS! WE'RE COMING TO SOMETHING...

LOOK AT THAT PORTRAIT! I CAN'T BELIEVE THE RUMORS ARE TRUE!

RUMORS?

SUN D'ARC DIDN'T STEAL THE MUMMY...

CHAPTER SIX:
DEADLINE AT MIDNIGHT

I'M SICK OF THAT STUPID *CURSE* THAT FORCES ME TO RETURN TO THE SARCOPHAGUS BY *MIDNIGHT* OR BECOME A *MUMMY* AGAIN.

I KNEW THAT IF WE SEARCHED *EVERY HIGH SCHOOL*, WE'D FIND A BOY WHO WOULD BE THE *PERFECT SUBSTITUTE* FOR YOU IN THE SARCOPHAGUS.

FIRST, WE HAVE TO REMOVE THE BOY'S *HEART* AND TAKE OUT HIS *BRAINS* THROUGH HIS *NOSTRILS*, AS WAS DONE TO YOU WHEN *YOU* WERE MUMMIFIED.

THAT'S WHY YOU'RE *HEARTLESS* AND *BRAINLESS*.

Hmph.
HEART AND BRAINS, WHO *NEEDS* 'EM?

JUST REMEMBER, IT WAS *ME*, THE BRILLIANT SCIENTIST, *DR. VORSCHAK*, WHO FIGURED OUT HOW TO BRING YOU BACK TO LIFE--AND *KEEP* YOU ALIVE--WITH MY SPECIAL *TANNA LEAF TEA*.

AND NOW THAT YOU'RE THE FAMOUS ROCK STAR *SUN D'ARC*, I GET HALF OF *EVERYTHING* YOU MAKE.

THIS ISN'T MAGIC ANYMORE--IT'S *SCIENCE!*

45

I KNEW SHE LOOKED FAMILIAR!

I JUST WISH YOU'D GIVEN ME A BETTER *NAME*. I WAS A GREAT EGYPTIAN PRINCE. I WANNA BE CALLED *PRINCE*.

THAT NAME WAS *TAKEN*.

BETTER GET STARTED. THIS PROCEDURE HAS TO BE FINISHED BY *MIDNIGHT*.

MEANWHILE...

ALMOST FORGOT. TIME TO DIAL WILLIAM AGAIN.

text text text

KICK

ALLOW ME. I'M TRAINED FOR THIS!

FOOLISH MORTAL. I DO NOT FEEL PAIN.

IT'S ALMOST *MIDNIGHT.* NO TIME TO TAKE OUT ANYBODY'S HEART AND BRAINS *TONIGHT.*

I DON'T WANT TO *GO BACK* INTO THAT *STUPID SARCOPHAGUS!*

NOT TO WORRY. THE FORMULA IN THESE INSTRUCTIONS WILL KEEP YOU OUT OF THE SARCOPHAGUS, AS LONG AS WILLIAM *REMAINS INSIDE* IT.

TOMORROW WE'LL REMOVE *EVERYBODY'S* BRAINS AND HEARTS. WE'LL FIND SOME EMPTY SARCOPHAGUSES FOR THE GIRLS.

Ahem

O SUN! ONCE SO BRIGHT, NOW ALL DRIED UP AND YUCKY, I WON'T FORGET YOU.

Sob

HUH? WHAT *HAPPENED?*

OH, HI, PRINCE.

IN HE *GOES.*

Sigh GUESS THAT'S WHERE HE *BELONGS* NOW.

THAT'S WHERE HE *ALWAYS* BELONGED.

GEE, HE'S *LIGHT* AS A *FEATHER.*

MOST MUMMIES ARE.

POUF

I'VE KNOWN A LOT OF MUMMIES.

ANYBODY MIND TELLING ME WHAT'S GOING ON?

EXPLAINING WILL TAKE ALL NIGHT. IN THE MEANTIME, CARE TO HELP PUT THIS LID BACK ON?

Huff!

EASY NOW, EASY!

Unngh A LITTLE... TO THE... LEFT...

WHOAH!

IT WEIGHS ABOUT A ZILLION POUNDS *MORE* THAN THE MUMMY.

CLICK

Us dogs have a good sense of balance.

I'LL *MISS* HIM...

The case of the Purloined Prince is solved.

I'M PHONING THE *MUSEUM* AND THE *EGYPTIAN ANTIQUITIES DEPARTMENT*. THEY'LL SEND SOMEONE TO COME AND GET RA-HOTEP.

InforFACEtion

Location: Behind the counter of Hernandez & Sons Pet Supplies

Hours: 9–5 during summer vacation. During the rest of the year, afterschool hours, except on weekends

Proprietor: Raf Hernandez (that's me) because it's my mom's store

Our motto:
Stumped? Scared? Need help fast?
Chicagoland Detectives:
We can do the job!

The Chicagoland Detective Agency is here for you. We solve low crimes and misdemeanors, and we battle injustice. Don't be afraid to come in with your pets. We love animals.

Friendly FACErs

3 Friends

Bradley

Megan Yamamura

William Johnson

Meet the FACE

Raf Hernandez
Age: 12
Education: James A. Garfield Middle School

Chicagoland BLOG ENTRY #2 ⊠

LET'S TALK MUMMIES!

The Chicagoland Detective Agency just solved a big case that involved antiquities smuggling and Egyptology. The mummy of the teen king Sun D'Arc was a huge part of the case.

The Egyptians preserved the bodies of their dead so that the dead could enjoy an afterlife in the Heavenly Fields. This afterlife was supposed to be just like their life on Earth, only better. So the kings and queens and rich people were buried along with little statues of servants, who would continue to serve them in the afterlife. This worked out fine if you were royalty or nobility, but wasn't so hot for the servants, who just continued to be servants forever. So hardly a democracy, no. continue...

Sun D'Arc ⊠

Ra-Hotep ⊠

They say the goddess Isis invented mummification when she mummified the body of her husband, the god Osiris, after he was killed by his jealous brother Seth. Isis must have loved Osiris A LOT and also must have had a strong stomach, because the mummification process is pretty gross. Usually it was NOT performed by wives on their husbands, but was done by professional embalmers.

First, the embalmers pulled out the brains of the dead person through the nostrils. Then they cut open the body and removed the internal organs: the lungs, the liver, the kidneys, the intestines, and the heart. They soaked all those pieces in a kind of salt solution called natron for 40 days. After that, they wrapped up each organ like a little mummy and put it in its own little mummy case or jar.

Are you grossed out yet?

Meanwhile, the embalmers were doing the same thing with the body, soaking it in natron for 40 days until it was dehydrated, then stuffing it with linen and spices, and wrapping it up in more long strips of linen. During this time, professional mourners, hired for the job, would wander the streets shrieking, beating their breasts, pretending to pull out their hair, and pouring dust on their heads.

Sun D'Arc: Ra-Hotep! ⊠

So maybe the mummies didn't wind up living again (except for some of them), but all that pulling out of brains and salting of livers turned out to be a good thing after all. Now scientists can examine 2,000-year-old mummies and find out all sorts of cool stuff about life in ancient Egypt. Such as what killed the famous teen king Tutankhamen, whose name means something like "the living image of the hidden sun god." Turns out the poor guy probably had all sorts of things wrong with him, including a cleft palate and a clubfoot, so he may have had to walk with a cane (he had a huge collection of them). But what killed him was likely malaria. Not murder, like some people used to think. It took a lot of detective work to find out all these things about someone who lived over 3,300 years ago.

Remember, the Chicagoland Detective Agency (chicagolanddetectiveagency.com) can find out all sorts of other cool stuff for you. You can find me behind the counter at Hernandez & Sons Pet Supplies weekdays after 3. We barter!

---

2 COMMENTS:

 Megan Yamamura A word or two about the ancient Egyptians that my esteemed colleague missed: they wore AWESOME makeup! They practically invented eye makeup. In fact, they probably DID invent eye makeup. That black stuff they lined their eyes with is called kohl, and it helped prevent eye infections. As soon as my extremely conservative dad, who mistakenly thinks 13 is too young, lets me, I will get some modern eyeliner and make up my eyes exactly like they did and, in fact, the way I did in my past life when I was Nefertiti, queen of Egypt.

My dark eyes recall
Past life as Nefertiti,
I must wear kohl NOW!
September 25 at 1:15 PM

 Bradley Personally, I think the ancient Egyptians were overrated. These guys worshipped—*are you ready?*—CATS! Cats were so important to them that when the family cat died, everybody would shave their eyebrows! They even turned their cats into little cat mummies!

But what about dogs? Did they worship dogs? When the faithful household doggie, man and woman's best friend, went to the Great Frisbee in the Sky, did they turn the little guy into a mummy? Did they shave their eyebrows? Not a chance!

Bunch of losers.
September 26 at 4:45 PM

TRINA ROBBINS, an Eisner Award and Harvey Award nominee, made a name for herself in the underground comix movement of the 1960s. She published the first all-woman comic book in the 1970s; published her first history of women cartoonists, *Women and the Comics*, in the 1980s; was an artist for the *Wonder Woman* comic book; and created the superhero series *Go Girl!* with artist Anne Timmons. And that's just a start—she has written biographies, other nonfiction, and way too many other books and comics for kids and adults to list, but you can check them out on her website at www.trinarobbins.com. She lives in San Francisco with her partner, comics artist Steve Leialoha.

TYLER PAGE is an Eisner Award-nominated illustrator and webcomic artist who has self-published four graphic novels, including *Nothing Better*, recipient of a Xeric Foundation Grant. His day job is director of Print Technology at the Minneapolis College of Art and Design, where he oversees the college's print-based facilities. He's been drawing his whole life, and sometime around middle school started making his own comics starring the family cat. He lives with wife Cori Doerrfeld, daughter Charlotte, and two crazy cats in Minneapolis, and his website lives at www.stylishvittles.com.

STUMPED? SCARED? NEED HELP FAST?

CHICAGOLAND
DETECTIVE AGENCY
CAN DO THE JOB.
NO CASE TOO WEIRD!

The word is out that Megan, Raf, and Raf's talking dog
Bradley are the team to go to when even weirder things
than usual start happening in Chicagoland. The Chicagoland
Detective Agency takes danger in hand (and paw) to find a
mysteriously missing puppy and an even more mysterious
pack of dogs that only shows up once a month.

Bradley can tell from the start: this is more than a simple
case of stray pets...and a whole lot more than a stray case
of full-moon transmogrification! Can high tech and haikus
save them all from the world's worst case of doggy breath?

The mystery will be chased down in...

CHICAGOLAND DETECTIVE AGENCY #3
NIGHT OF THE LIVING DOGS

BY TRINA ROBBINS
ILLUSTRATED BY TYLER PAGE